JOSEPH LOVES JULIETTE

THE MASTERSON SERIES BOOK FIVE

LISA LANG BLAKENEY

WRITERGIRL PRESS

LISA LANG BLAKENEY

Love reading novels featuring hot alpha men who fall for smart women? Then join <u>MY VIP MAILING LIST</u> at http://LisaLangBlakeney.com/VIP and get a free book just for joining!

FOLLOW ME
Follow me on Facebook
Join my Fan Group
Follow me on Amazon
Follow me on Bookbub
Follow me on Instagram
Follow me on TikTok

CONTENTS

Claimed - Camden & Jade

Indebted - Cutter & Sloan

Broken - Stone & Tiny

Promised - All King Brothers

King Brothers Box Set

The Nighthawk Series

Sexy & sweet sports romances set in the professional world of football. All standalones.

Saint - Saint & Sabrina

Wolf - Cooper & Ursula

Diesel - Mason & Olivia

Jett - Jett & Adrienne

Rush - Rush & Mia

AUTHOR'S NOTE

Hi Fabulous Readers!

This is a short & sweet one featuring the *instalove* and fated connection between self-made billionaire Joseph Masterson and Juliette Hill. These two are secondary characters in my bestselling Masterson Series featuring Joseph's son, Roman Masterson.

I wrote this story because many readers were interested in Joseph and Juliette's backstory. If you're a Joseph fan, I think you'll enjoy it! If you're new to me, then this will give you a glimpse into the intensity of the Masterson Men! (Some of my favorite alphas to write.)

INTRODUCTION

Whatever she wants.
Whenever she wants it.
However she likes it.

As teenagers, it was love at first sight for Joseph
Masterson and Juliette Hill, but they were from
completely different worlds and it wasn't meant to
be. When the two have a second chance meeting as
adults, they discover that the powerful chemistry
between them is still there and stronger than
ever. But this time there's no way he's letting her go.
In fact, this time, his mission is to give Juliette the
world or die trying.

JULIETTE

"Everyone has a moment that may change and ultimately shape their lives. The trick is realizing when it's happening. I know when mine occurred. It was twice. The first was the moment my eyes locked with Joseph Masterson's. The second was when he walked back into my living room and claimed my heart."

-Juliette Hill-Masterson

JOSEPH

Ode To Juliette

The very first moment I laid eyes on my wife I was dumbstruck. She was ethereal. A vision. The most beautiful girl I'd ever seen in my life or the next.

There were a million reasons why someone like me shouldn't have even bothered looking in Juliette Hill's direction, but I've never been a reasonable man.

I was raised in the gutter.

A boy from the streets.

And I've had to do a myriad of *unreasonable* things to get myself out of there, and even worse to stay out.

But I wouldn't change a thing.

Because every morning that I wake up to see and touch my wife's warm, luscious body laying next to mine–I am convinced that everything that I've done has been worth it.

There was no way that the innocent girl I met, and the sophisticated woman that she's grown to be, would have ever settled for anything less. Less than who I am. Who I've carved myself into.

So I'll do whatever. Eliminate whoever. Whatever it takes to make sure that my woman stays next to me. Warm in my bed. For the rest of the days I have left on this Godforsaken earth.

She is mine.

She is everything.

She is my Juliette.

**Franklin Senior High
A lifetime ago...**

My best friend Karen is running down the second floor hallway towards me at warp speed in her washed out Billy Idol T-shirt, with her freshly dyed punk rock pink highlights flying wildly behind her.

Any other day I would have been chuckling at her pigeon toed gallop, but today seems different. I can tell by the look of urgency in her eyes that something is seriously wrong, and that she's dying to tell me whatever it is.

A knot begins to slowly form in the pit of my empty stomach, and it's not because I skipped breakfast. I can tell that this isn't going to be a dose of our usual mindless morning gossip. Something's very wrong.

She calls out to me with urgency. "Jules!"

I'm momentarily relieved that she is at least still calling me by my nickname, so it must not be all that bad. If someone was seriously hurt then she would call me by my full name, *Juliette*, but my eyes still grow wide with dreaded curiosity.

"What is it, Kay? What's wrong?"

"Let's go outside to The Pit. I need to ask you something."

Outside of school grounds, on the West side of Franklin Senior High School, is a self dedicated area for the kids in our school who smoke cigarettes and sometimes pot called The Pit.

At this time of day, mid-morning, it's a really good place to get away for a few moments of privacy. Most of the smokers are actually already in second period study hall, also known as the "do last night's homework" period, so we'll basically have the area to ourselves. We're skipping gym, which is fine, since we have a substitute teacher all week.

Karen takes a deep breath and a long swallow in what seems an effort to stall, but because of the lump forming in my throat, I simply wait silently and patiently for her to gather her composure and say whatever it is. Honestly, she's scaring the shit out of me. She never acts like this.

"So…are things still good with David?"

"Yes…why?" I ask hesitantly. Afraid of where this may be going.

"So you talk to him still…I mean you two are still together?"

I'm getting freaked out by all the questions. Karen knows damn well that we are together, but obviously she knows something about David that I don't. I just wish she would spit it out already.

"Yes, Kay, you know we're still together. What. Is. It?"

Karen nervously rubs her hands up and down the front of her pants as she continues on.

"Well…I heard from someone that you had s.e.x. with him last weekend."

My stomach drops as she spells out the word.

S.E.X.

How does she know.

"What," I respond in a pained voice.

"Of course that isn't true… right?"

"Who told you that?"

"Well is it true?" she asks incredulously. "Did you give up your *not-until-I-meet-my-husband* virginity to David and not even tell your best friend about it?"

I might have mentioned to Karen that I was going to wait until I met and married my husband before having sex. That I promised my parents and my priest that I wouldn't. Actually I might have told her that a thousand times. How could I not? It's been drilled into me by my irrationally conservative and judgmental mother since I got my first period.

Keep your legs closed, Juliette. Premarital sex is a sin against God. Plus you don't want to end up like your Aunt Tina. She should have never had a kid without getting married first. That unemployed boyfriend of hers left her high and dry before the baby even took her first breath. There's a place in hell for deadbeat fathers like him.

So ever since I can remember, abstinence until marriage was my motto. A plan to assure me that I would never disgrace the family or myself like poor Aunt Tina did, but then I second guessed all of that when I fell for David, or at least my hormones did all the second guessing for me.

"I want to know who told you that." I demand an answer. Choosing to ignore Karen's hissy fit about not *knowing* first, because that's totally besides the point.

"Gosh, it is true!" she exclaims with a mixture of awe and anger. "Well, you're not going to like this, but Sarah Dixon was the one who told me that you had sex with David. She said she found out, because her stupid brother saw the whole thing."

I'm just about ten seconds away from vomiting all over The Pit's azalea bushes.

Her brother saw me having sex?

Saw!

Sarah is a popular senior at Franklin and has a big mouth that runs incessantly about whatever gossip is flying around that day. Her twin brother is a friend of David's. If those two know, then I have little doubt that the entire school knows or will know very soon that I've lost my virginity.

"What do you mean he saw?" I whisper the question as if speaking it quietly will make his crime any less of a possibility.

"Don't freak out, but evidently David must have told Sarah's brother and some other guys that you were coming over his house last weekend and what the *plan* was."

She says the word *plan* using air quotes.

"So according to Sarah, they came over before you got there and hid in his walk-in closet. I think they watched everything, Jules. Those spoiled assholes."

I try to stop them from falling, but it's difficult. Heavy, salty, tears start to roll down my face, and then an excruciating tightness in my throat and chest forms that I pray will be the death of me.

Heart attack at seventeen.

Just kill me and get it over with.

I'll never be able to hold my head up in this school again. I can honestly say that I probably don't hate anyone on earth as much as I hate David right now.

"How many people know?" I ask softly.

"I don't really know, but it wasn't like Sarah's brother actually told her. She overheard him talking to someone on the phone, making fun of the fact that David only lasted three minutes before he … well you know….came.

"But I don't think they're going around telling tons of people though," she says quickly. "You're not some hoe bag, Jules. They know that. They were laughing more at him than you."

I close my eyes for several moments as the realization hits me that there were other people in the room. Guys that definitely know who I am and who all of my friends are. Guys who probably saw every face I made. Heard every noise I made. Heard me say that I loved him. Guys who have big mouths.

People don't necessarily know that I'm not a hoe bag or some skank. If those guys start running their mouths, kids will start talking about me over casual lunch conversation with their friends, and the story will take on a life of its own. I know because I've seen it happen to other girls in my school. David may have single-handedly ruined my reputation in the only place I've ever lived. In the only place I've ever known.

Now that I think closely back on that night, I remember the closet. I remember thinking how nice David's professionally decorated bedroom was. He had high cathedral ceilings with a professionally painted mural of the seashore on one wall, expensive dark mahogany wood furniture with brass pulls, and there were these cool, intricately carved double doors to his closet, which now when I think about it were slightly ajar that day.

I didn't think anything about it at the time. I certainly didn't think they were open so that people could watch one of the only moments in my life that I'll never get to do over.

I lower my head in quiet shock and disbelief as it all really begins to sink in. Karen begins gently rubbing her hand up and down my back and staring at me with caution, like she is waiting for me to erupt or have a nervous breakdown or something.

While the tears are already starting to roll down my face, I still haven't broken out in the "ugly cry" yet, and I am trying my damnedest not to let it get to that point. Not because Karen hasn't ever seen me break down, she has most definitely seen it once or twice, but I guess I'm trying to convince myself that I'll be all right.

Although I'm not sure that I will be fine at all.

Not ever again.

I really like David.

What I mean is that I really *liked* David.

He moved to our town when we were both starting the fifth grade, so we've known each other a long time. We were always friendly, but he never paid me much attention until last year.

It was then that he started looking at me differently: flirting with me in English class, sitting next to me in the lunchroom, holding my hand in the hallways. I guess that's what hurts most about this. I thought I knew him, but I didn't see this coming—not by a long shot.

"Shows you what I know," I say to Karen. I attempt to smile in jest, but it ends up being more of a painful smirk. "I thought him lasting three minutes before it was over was a good thing."

I can see what can only be described as pity slowly clouding my friend's eyes. She has to be thinking what I already know–that David thinks that I'm a joke. That our "relationship" was all in my head, and that I'm an idiot, and that there is no way those guys, whoever they are, aren't going around telling everybody about what they saw.

The kids in our school are notorious for spreading gossip in record time, so I can pretty much be assured that everyone will know that I am no longer a virgin as well as the color of my frickin' underwear by the end of the week.

I'm finally beginning to process the enormity of everything Karen has just told me, and it's probably the cause of the throbbing pain at the base of my head.

I'm doomed.

I pinch the sides of my neck firmly to alleviate some pressure then slump down defeatedly on the wooden bench behind me, drop my books, and start to sob.

Here it finally comes.

The ugly cry.

Karen immediately sits down next to me and

wraps one of her arms around my shoulders. It's a rare show of affection from my tough as nails bestie, which is why I appreciate it so much.

"It's going to be fine, Jules. It was your first time. You held out for the guy you thought was the one. How many girls in the senior class, hell…in this entire school can say that? Most of them gave it up eons ago. Myself included."

Karen flashes me a warm grin which soothes some of the ache I feel in my heart. Maybe she is at least partially right. Perhaps I can take some solace in the fact that I definitely was one of the last mohicans when it came to losing my virginity. No one I know is in any position to judge me.

Right?

"I thought it was special…I thought he at least respected me…He took me out for pancakes afterwards. Oh my God, I sound ridiculous don't I? He's a jerk…I knew this already…I've seen him with other girls…Why would I sleep with him, Karen?"

"Because he is one of the most popular guys in school and he's always been nice to you. How were you supposed to know that he would pull something this heinous. Who makes a plan to have their friends watch them having sex. I mean *who* does that?!"

I love and appreciate that Karen is just as angry and appalled as I am. Like always, she has my back.

"Who else was there?" I needed to know.

Karen hesitated.

"Could this get any worse? Just tell me. I want to know who's walking around talking about me behind my back."

"I need to ask first. Did you at least enjoy it? If you had given me a heads up that you were going to do it, I would have given you some pointers."

"It was supposed to be a private moment between the two of us. You're going to need to get over the fact that I didn't tell you," I say a little irritated. She just comforted me two-seconds ago, and now she's finding a way to make this about herself.

"My bad, Jules, you're a hundred percent right."

"And as far as if I enjoyed it—was I whooping and hollering like you claim you do all the time? Uh, no. It was three minutes of him grunting and me holding my breath until he was finished."

"Yikes."

"Exactly—I think you and a thousand Rated R movies lied to me about how wonderful sex supposedly is."

"Well, it's hard to have an orgasm the first go 'round."

I have no interest in talking orgasms or technique. I just want to hear the rest of the details about what happened in that room. I need to know what I'm dealing with.

"Who else was there, Kay? That's all I care about. Whose car windows am I bashing out tonight?"

Like I really have the balls to knock someone's windows out. My brothers probably would, but there's no way I'm ever telling them about this, mainly because they would yell at me first for being so stupid and sleeping with David.

"There was Sarah's brother Ray and two other kids with him I think."

"Who are they?"

"I don't know, but I don't think they're from here. If you're going to stress at all, I think Ray is the one that we have to worry about keeping his trap shut. I mean that is if you're even worried at all."

If I'm worried? Is she serious? Clearly Karen must be trying some reverse psychology crap we learned in class to trick me into believing that this isn't a big deal.

It isn't working.

"You had sex with your *boyfriend,* Jules," she continues talking. "Three people saw. So what?! Hell, you didn't murder someone. You didn't sleep with all three of them (not that I'm slut shaming), but it's just not that big of a deal if you ask me."

While I appreciate my best friend's attempt to downplay this catastrophe, I know what she's saying is pure and utter nonsense.

"If it wasn't that big of deal, Kay, you wouldn't have skipped class to find me and tell me like it was a matter of life or death. You know it's a big deal. We hang in a small enough circle that everyone is going to find out and everyone is going to talk. Same thing happened to Marion last year, and you see what happened to her."

"You and Marion are two very different people."

"Are we? Kids are going to make me out to be the dumb, naive girl who got herself entangled with the 'out of my league' quarterback. It's all so cliche."

"Oh please, you watch too much television. This is just an arrogant jock, with a huge ego, taking advantage of his sweet and trusting girlfriend. I never had him pegged for being capable of doing something this slimy, but sometimes people lose their minds when it comes to sex. I think that's why so many people on this planet are into porn. I've got a juicy book to show you by the way. It's loaded with freaky sex scenes."

"No, thank you. I've come to the conclusion that

sex is overrated and should only be used for procreation."

"What?! I know it seems that way to you now, but sex is actually a whole lot of fun when it's with the right person."

"And you know this how? Through experience, Dr. Ruth?" I ask incredulously. "Look, I thought I had the right person, and like I said before, it was overrated. Look at what a mess having sex with him one frickin' time caused me already."

A freshman girl starts to walk over towards us. She's looking mostly at me, and I start to think crazy thoughts–like perhaps she knows about what happened between David and me.

"Keep it moving, freshman," Karen orders.

Her eyes bulge in what I think is a combination of surprise and fright, but then she silently pivots and starts walking in another direction.

"Do you think she knows?" I ask Karen.

"You're being paranoid. She knows nothing. She just wanted to check out the pit like every other underclassman."

Freshmen and sophomores aren't allowed in the pit. It's not an actual school rule, but rather a social construct created by juniors and seniors of our high school long before our time here.

"She was staring at me."

"Because all of the freshmen know who we are, Jules. We're seniors. I'm the loud one. You're the pretty one. I'm a badass–"

"And I'm notorious."

Karen rolls her eyes.

"You are not."

"I hate the guys in this town."

"Yeah, sometimes they can be straight up douchebags, but what's a Penn Washington girl to do? Until we escape this town, they're all we've got."

"Not for me."

"So you're never going to date? Never going to have sex again? You'd only be punishing yourself, Jules."

"Well, it's a punishment which I'll gladly accept."

JULIETTE

For the rest of the morning I move from AP English, to gym, and to calculus basically numb. The only thing I was paying attention to was the fact that just as I suspected, gossip moves lightening fast through our school, and certain girls were staring at me out of the sides of their eyes.

This isn't me being paranoid.

This is real.

They know.

I take special notice of the smug stares of two girls that I have been longtime frenemies with–Carla Ritter and Marie Puzzini. Two ringleaders of a group of girls who have what Karen has coined *The*

Franklin Package: bad attitudes, big mouths, and parents with money. These girls love running people's names through the mud. They did it to poor Marion until she couldn't take anymore and switched to another high school.

Now don't misunderstand me, I realize that we aren't living in the nineteenth century or anything. Obviously I'm not a whore just because I had sex one time with David, but it's the fact that there are witnesses. That he permitted them to watch as if it were a peep show. Like it meant nothing to him. Like *I* mean absolutely nothing.

Karen tried to reassure me throughout the day by passing me folded notes, sealed with smiley faces, that everything is going to be okay and that barely anyone knows or cares about my night with David. I don't think she is telling me the complete truth though, but it doesn't matter. I truly appreciate her effort to make me feel better.

In fact in some small way, I now feel guilty that I didn't share my momentous, once in a lifetime news with her first, and that she had to hear about it through a second hand source. Especially because she called me right away and told me about her first time with her boyfriend, Bobby Wagner, when we were sophomores.

I'm not exactly sure why I didn't tell her. Maybe because as soon as David and I were finished–I regretted it. Having sex was not something I necessarily was dying to have, but it was more like something I wanted to check off my list. Something that was a right of passage. Something that David had been asking for repeatedly. In other words, I did it for all the wrong reasons just as my mother feared I would.

Today is an early dismissal day for seniors. I usually stay after school and work on college applications in the library, but today I've decided to head home for the obvious reasons. I plan on crawling into a pint of butter pecan ice cream and then into my bed until graduation day.

I'm only midway down the school's old stone staircase when I spot the very last person that I want to see is waiting for me.

It's the jerk.

"What do you want?" I ask coolly.

"Jules."

I can tell by the hesitance in his voice that he suspects that I already know what he's done. He isn't his usual confident, cocky, self.

"What's up?" I ask with a hand on my hip and the

corner of my mouth turned up in an accusatory manner.

David pauses like cowards often do when they're about to lie.

"Uh, I wanted to talk to you."

He steps closer to me.

I step back.

To further understand the depth of my mistake, David is "the man" at our high school. He's the football team's quarterback, an honor society student, good looking, and while I'm now ashamed to even admit it–I felt more important when I walked the halls with him. Now his close proximity just makes me feel sick to my stomach.

"About?"

"Stories floating around about us that aren't necessarily true."

Necessarily? Is he kidding me?

"There's not a single frickin' thing I want to discuss with you, David."

"Jules…just give me five minutes."

"You really want to do this in front of school?"

I inadvertently raise my voice a littler louder than I intended, so I turn to check to see if anyone is close enough to hear our conversation. David doesn't flinch.

"I just want to talk."

"There's nothing to say. Were your friends trying to decide who'd get the next crack at me? Is watching girls your thing? Do you charge admission for deflowering virgins?"

I am so angry that I want to cry, but I hate exhibiting huge emotions in front of people. I've already cried once today in front of Karen, and so I refuse to do it again. My throat tightens as I take a long hard swallow and use all my inner strength to hold the sniffles back. I don't want to give the imbecile the satisfaction.

"Calm down, Jules. Let me explain."

"Explain what? Why you treated me like a whore? I mean I should have known better right? You made it quite clear that you weren't totally sold on this whole girlfriend/boyfriend thing anyway. Remember you told me that?"

"I said that months ago."

"Well, now you can rest easy that you don't have to worry about that anymore. I don't want you. We're done, David."

"But I'm not ready to end it."

Delusional douchebag alert.

"Oh it's ended. We're done. Tada the frickin' end."

A few students, who have been circling around us

like buzzards, overhear my words and start to chuckle. Immediately David's posture changes. His back stiffens and his eyes grow colder than I've ever seen them.

"You gave me *gonorrhea*." He makes sure to say the last word of his declaration loud enough so that everyone within earshot can hear.

More students start to gather around us. All I see are kids I've passed by in the hallways all my life with their eyes bulged wide and hands up to their mouths in morbid curiosity.

"That's impossible," I say defiantly. Determined to defend my reputation.

"You're the only one I've been with. I *definitely* got it from you."

I look around at the crowd continuing to swell. I catch a glimpse of disgust on a boy's face that I've never seen before. Just as I feared, I am the victim in all of this and David is the one who is going to come out smelling like a rose.

I wish the ground would crack open and swallow me whole.

I am shaken.

I am mortified.

He has ruined me.

"I was a virgin, you asshole!" I say before the tears start to fall. "You are the only one I've been with. I didn't give you anything."

Except my heart.

And then I take off running.

JULIETTE

’m barely past the parking lot when I realize that I don't have my coin purse which is usually attached to my bookbag by a small silver keyring.

It's odd that I don't have it, and I can't find it anywhere which is not a good thing, because my entire life is in there: my student ID, twenty-three dollars that my dad gave me this morning, and my driver's license.

I sit on the edge of the curb and rummage through my bag. Maybe I forgot and dropped it inside. Maybe it's buried down below with my assortment of ballpoint pens and tampons.

Crapola.

It's not here.

I can't believe this, but I'm going to have to turn around and head back to school to find it. As I very slowly make my way back towards the building, I finally remember what I did with it.

I actually detached my change purse from my bag and dropped it off at my locker in between classes. I didn't recall what I'd done at first, because I've been like a zombie the entire day. Hell, I'm still a zombie.

I'm only a few steps away from the main entrance when I hear a commotion brewing. I'd hoped that the crowd had dispersed after our little show was over but no such luck. As I approach, it's almost like a scene out of a primetime teen drama.

The same crowd of students who overhead my conversation with David, are still gathered around the base of the front steps. Several of them turn their heads and stare at me with condemnatory faces as I approach. It isn't until one brave soul (a guy from my study hall) approaches me that I finally discover what's going on.

"David was just beaten up. He's behind the school and he looks kind of bad."

"What?! Show me."

It only takes me a few seconds to jog around to the back of the school, and that's when I see him.

Sprawled out on his back, with a bloody eye, and clutching his side as if he's in severe pain.

A few of his teammates are standing around him, but I manage to push my way through the circle with a few curt *excuse me's* and *pardon me's*, and I almost clutch my pearls once I see his battered face.

His lip is split and his left eye seems to be already turning purple and puffy. After I release a small gasp, horrified by what I see, I bend down and gently touched the side of his face. I may hate him, but I'm still a human being capable of empathy.

"Did anyone call the paramedics?" I ask any and everyone standing around.

"We did," one of his teammates confirms.

"David…David, can you hear me?" I ask with slight urgency. His eyes are closed and he's not moving much.

I check his pockets and notice that his wallet, keys, and several folded twenty dollar bills are still there, so this isn't some sort of robbery. Not that I actually thought that he'd been robbed on our quiet, suburban campus, but now I'm really baffled, because that means that he has been targeted.

Did one of his friends do this?

I look back up at the five large bodies standing around me. All of them play football with David, and

I suspect that at least one of them was probably in that closet watching me have sex.

"Why are you all just standing here?" I ask. "Did one of you do this to him? Do you know who did?"

Nothing.

No one says a word.

They all just stare at me with these blank expressions on their faces.

"David, can you open your eyes?"

Finally I start to see his one good eyelid flutter and his fingers move.

He winces in pain.

"Jules?" His voice croaks.

"Yes, I'm here," I respond.

While I'm relieved that he is at least awake and slightly coherent, now that I have confirmation that David isn't dead, I have some fleeting not-so-nice thoughts about him.

This is what you get for being a complete jerk and embarrassing me in front of the entire school.

This is what you get for lying to me.

This is what you get for letting people watch me in your bedroom.

This is what you get for trying to ruin my reputation.

I hope you're in lots of pain, jackass.

I am definitely a firm believer in karmic justice,

and I have no doubt that karma is responsible for the fact that David's been beaten to a pulp after casting me as an unwilling participant of his own little peep show. God doesn't like ugly.

"Help is coming soon," I say flatly. "Your so-called friends here said they called 911."

"Listen to me," he says almost urgently as he grimaces through the pain, but this is no time for apologies. I don't want to hear it.

"Quiet," I silence him. "Talk later."

He grabs my forearm. "Wait, Jules, the guy that did this–"

I should have realized when I first came upon David sprawled across the ground that something more was off. It's weird that his teammates are all just standing around waiting for an ambulance. No one was actually doing anything. No one even went back into the school to get him an ice pack or some-thing. It was like they were too frightened to do anything to help.

"Stand up."

I'm still bent down by David's side when I whip my head around and stare towards the direction of the deep, dangerous voice that just startled me.

The crowd of footballers parts with ease as the tall stranger approaches.

I remember his face.

He was the boy staring at me with disgust on his face when David and I were arguing.

"Are you talking to me?" I manage to eke out.

"Yes–and I told you to stand up and walk away."

My eyes enlarge at his direct words and his crude manner. I feel like a deer caught in a pair of blinding headlights. Frightened to move. Unable to budge from my spot on the ground. The stranger holds my stare with his threatening jet black irises and wills me to my feet with them.

I rise to a standing position slowly, determined to face this beautiful but lethal looking boy. No wait, he's more man than boy. I can surmise that underneath his clothes, every muscle in his body is sleekly defined, and he's so tall that I could literally climb him like a pole and see for miles around.

Dressed in dark indigo blue jeans, a blue t-shirt, worn black leather boots, and tons of attitude leaking from his pores–he definitely gives off a mature type of energy.

A masculine, tough, raw, dominant kind of energy.

The kind of energy that clouds your mind and demands that you to listen to everything that its owner has to say.

It's obvious that he doesn't belong to this school or probably to this town. I've never seen anyone like him before in my life, and he is definitely someone who is unforgettable. This is a guy who could walk down the street and everyone would take notice. In fact, everyone is staring at him right now.

"Who are you?" I ask almost in awe.

"That's the douchebag who did this to me," David warns through painful groans from the ground. "Get away from him, Jules!"

"Why'd you come back here?" the stranger asks in an almost accusatory manner. His eyes relentlessly holding mine with an unsettling laser focus. Totally ignoring David's claims.

"I forgot my wallet," I answer reservedly. Intimidated by the tone of his voice yet strangely attracted to it at the same time.

"Where is it?"

"Umm, I think I left it in my locker."

"Let's go to your locker then."

For a moment my feet almost mindlessly follow the stranger's directive, but then finally my brain kicks in. Who is this guy? How old is he? Where is he from? Why is he going around beating up high school students, and why am I listening to everything he says?

I look around at the spectators as if I'm going to find an explanation or at least an ally. All I see are many familiar faces but no real friends.

Karen is a violinist and has orchestra everyday after school, so I don't expect to see her, but finally I do spot the guy from study hall again. He silently nods his head no to me. I'm not exactly sure what the nod means though. Is he trying to warn me against listening to the stranger or against defying him?

I cock my head to the side and look at study hall guy a little more intently. Silently willing him to give me another hint as to what he's trying to communicate.

"Is there a problem?" the stranger asks after noticing the non verbal exchange between the two of us. Study hall guy averts his eyes away and down to the ground, and now I'm seriously starting to worry.

Everyone seems terrified of this guy. I guess the condition of David's face might be the reason why. We don't see many fights at our school.

I'm kind of wishing that either one of my older brothers still attended high school and were here to step in, but when I notice Principal Pike walking his way towards the group, that's when I make a split second decision. I don't want the stranger to have to deal with our by-the-book principal.

I can only assume by the evidence that he is indeed the person who hit David, and that he may have possibly done it for me. I also can assume that he is over eighteen years old and could face serious legal consequences if the principal involves the police. So I am making the decision to protect him.

"No, there's no problem."

"Dummy," David says to me from the ground.

"Say another fucking word," the stranger says in a menacing voice to David. "I dare you."

David doesn't speak again, but his eyes are shooting daggers straight through me. If I were a voodoo doll, I'd have pins stuck in very painful places based on the hate emanating from his glare.

"Let's go," the stranger orders.

I give David one last look and start walking towards the front entrance of the school. I keep my eyes focused downwards as a way of hiding from Principal Pike as we pass each other. I've done nothing wrong, but the fact that I may bare some responsibility for the football star's face looking like a bloody ribeye makes me feel as if I'm in some way culpable.

As we head back toward the building, my stomach is in knots. The stranger is walking very close to me, yet he seems to be very careful about not taking large steps ahead of me. Our arms brush dangerously close to each other but never touch.

Still…my skin tingles.

"Do we know each other?" I ask as we walk inside of the building. More curious than ever as to why a boy like this would take any interest in a girl like me.

"No."

"Are you sure?"

"No one could never forget a face like yours. So yes, I'm positive that we don't know each other."

My cheeks grow flushed. I'm not very used to compliments, not unless they're from family members, but I think I could start to get very used to them.

Several kids are still at school for various after school activities, and they stare almost with awe at us as we pass through the hallway. Without having to say a word, they move completely out of our way, and it's pretty obvious why.

The stranger has an ominous presence about him. A dangerous energy which rolls off of him in waves with each calculated stride he takes through the building–yet I don't think that I'm in any danger. On the contrary, I've never felt more protected.

"Is that it?"

I'm relieved to open my locker and find my coin purse on the upper shelf inside.

"Yes."

"Good, let's go. Gonna make sure you get home."

The butterflies inside of me start crashing against

each other inside of me. I know better than to let some strange guy walk me home. It's not smart. Plus my brothers would kill me if they found out.

"Umm, I think I'll be okay to head home on my own."

He shuts my locker door closed.

"After the shit I saw and heard today, I'm driving you home. End of story."

"Driving?"

That's an even scarier proposition.

"My car is in the parking lot."

"I'm sorry, but I don't know you."

"Then let's get to know each other."

I glance across the hallway and notice that the library only has a few students inside. There's a particular alcove inside, where I usually like to read, that I think would be a good place for us to sit and away from prying eyes.

"Let's go sit in the library."

He hesitates for a moment then acquiesces.

"Okay."

"Umm, so did you used to go to this school?"

"This school?" he scoffs. "Hell, no."

"Okay, so I guess you have something against Penn Washington."

"I'm a city boy, but now that I've met you, I may have to reevaluate my prejudice against the 'burbs."

"We haven't really met though."

"Haven't we?"

Every single word he says sets off a tiny little firework inside of me. Something about the way he looks at me and talks to me makes me feel like a spectacular attraction.

"What's your name?" I finally ask. A question which I should've asked about ten minutes ago.

"Joseph."

A biblical name. My mother would like that.

Wait–what are you saying, crazy girl?

"Nice to meet you, Joseph, I'm Juliette."

He leans over with a fiercely intense look on his face. "Nice to formally meet you too, Juliette."

I get a good whiff of him. He smells subtly of cologne, strength, confidence, and freakin' wedding bells.

Oh my God, I'm losing it.

"Did you by chance have anything to do with David's busted eye?"

"David."

He repeats the name in a tone filled with malice and venom.

"Yes, the guy on the ground."

"I had everything to fucking do with it."

"So you heard everything that was said between us," I whisper.

"Yes, I heard everything."

Ground. Swallow. Me. Now.

I hang my head down.

"Oh."

Joseph leans forward and uses his hand to lift my chin up to meet his stone faced gaze.

"Don't ever look away from me or anybody else like you're ashamed, Juliette. You make decisions in this life, you own 'em. You slept with that dicktard once, but you won't make that mistake again."

My eyes get glassy.

"But you don't even know the worst part," I say.

"He let a couple of his creepy ass friends watch."

"Oh my God, you know about that too?!"

"People are stupid. They run their mouths about all types of unimportant shit to make their pathetic little lives seem better. It doesn't matter. Ain't shit you can do about it now but move on."

"You're right," I nod my head in agreement. "And I know what he did to me was awful, but I guess what I don't understand is why you took it upon yourself to get involved?"

"Because you're worth it."

I swallow nervously.

"What?"

"I'm a grown man, on a high school campus, and

I assaulted a student. Anything could have happened to me out there, anything could still happen when we leave this building, but I don't give a damn because you are worth it to me, Juliette. You are worth fighting for. Always remember that."

I don't know what to say to those powerful words. Words that I want to cling to like plastic wrap and keep fresh inside of me forever. Words that I know don't make a lot of sense considering that he is a complete stranger to me. Words that I should probably run from and not revel in.

"You don't know me," I practically whisper.

"You keep saying that, but I know all that I need to know. I know that you didn't deserve what happened to you, and I know that you're better than him. I can tell. I'm good at reading people. Although a blind man could tell that you are better than that asshat."

"Sometimes you speak like you're a thirty year old man."

"Do I?" He chuckles.

It's the first real smile I've seen him make. He has a captivating smile. An unforgettable smile. And like everything else about him, I'm drawn to it.

"How old are you, Joseph?"

"You ask a lot of questions."

"We have to get to know each other if you're going to drive me home."

"Are you flirting with me right now, Juliette?"

I swear his voice just dropped an octave.

"No."

"Liar."

"I think we better get going. I'm surprised no one has come in here looking for you yet."

"David doesn't have as many friends as he thinks. I don't think anyone out there is willing to rat me out after what he's done."

"I don't think you understand Penn Washington at all. They're probably laughing about what he did to me and running their mouths about you as we speak. They may have even called the police by now. Kids here are like that."

"I understand people, Juliette, and when given the right motivation they seem to do what you want them to do. Trust me, I feel very confident that we're going to walk out of those doors and into my car with no problem."

Umm, okay.

"So are you ready to let me take you home now?" he asks.

"Sure."

"Do we know each other well enough?" he teases.

"Yes," I smile almost forgetting about everything that's happened to me today. If just being around this boy enables me to block out some of the bad, I want to be around him just a bit longer.

"Let's go then."

Joseph stands up and starts walking towards the exit, and I follow right behind him. My heart racing the entire time. It thumps a few beats because I'm nervous about what could be waiting for him outside of those doors, and a few more beats totally just for how freakin' hot I think this guy is. I've never met anyone like him before, and he literally has my head spinning.

Where did he come from?

When we get outside I'm relived to find that the school's front steps are clear. No students, no principal, and no police. I pause once Joseph approaches a souped up black Camaro and motions to open the door for me. I've never been in a car like this. This looks fast and dangerous. My parents drive super safe Volvos.

"Do we need to talk longer?" he asks sensing my hesitation.

"I guess we could we talk a bit more while we drive," I say.

"Sounds good."

We both slide in our seats and he leans over me to reach for my seatbelt.

"Safety first," he quips.

I hold my breath as the back of his hand inadvertently brushes against my breasts as he slides the belt across and fastens me in.

"And Juliette–let's make sure to take the long way home."

JULIETTE

Six Years Later

It smells like snow. Like we're headed for a blanket of powder all over the beautiful Philadelphia suburb of Penn Washington. The place where my parents call home, and their parents, and as far as my mother is concerned–the place that our entire family are the founding fathers of.

It's also the place that I unfortunately have to call home when I'm not away at law school, although my hope is that I never have to move back here permanently.

My parents are in the middle of planning their annual New Year's Eve party, and my mother is freaking out about the impending snowstorm.

Every year the party gets a little larger, the guest lists grows, the decorations become a little more elaborate, and the hors d'oeuvres a little more expensive. All to impress a house full of people my family does business with or wants to do business with.

Lawyers.

They're a very particular bunch.

Elitists. Drunks. Geniuses. Cutthroats.

Every year, anyone who's anyone in the legal field in the Philadelphia area, comes to our house to brag about what they bought their significant other for Christmas, what their biggest case was for the year, what new car they plan on buying, and what new firm they're considering working for.

It's the same boring crap year after year, but it's in our blood. Every Hill for the last three generations has been a lawyer. Everyone but my youngest brother, but he's a court bailiff, so he's still in that world as far as I'm concerned–although my family begs to differ. They give him a lot of flack about his chosen profession. It's probably why they are riding me so hard.

Juliette, when are you going to take the bar?
Juliette, have you been studying?

Juliette, there's never been a Hill who didn't pass the Pennsylvania bar exam on the first try.

Gah!

The only good thing about these parties is that there's going to be lots of liquor. I'm going to need it. The only way not to succumb the rigorous questioning I'm going to have to endure tonight is to get totally and absolutely sloshed.

I walk over to my father who's hanging up some last minute light strings around the gazebo in the back yard.

"I'm not sure why you two don't hire someone to do this for you. You're going to break your sweet old neck if you keep this up, daddy," I say.

"You make total sense, sweet pea, but you know your mother is a complete control freak. She would just stand there and micromanage whoever she hired, so it's just better if I do it. At least she trusts me." He chuckles.

"I can go get one of the other step ladders and help you out, dad."

"Absolutely not, that's what your brothers are for. You're supposed to be inside doing your mother's bidding. You know the routine."

"Exactly," I mutter to myself. Then I speak

directly to my father. "I know exactly what she wants me to do, and that's why I'm out here."

"You can't hide from your mom forever. No one's safe when it comes to The Hill Family Party prep."

"I see that. She even has you, a court circuit judge, hanging Christmas lights."

My father stops what he's doing for a moment to ask me a question with a serious look spread across his face.

"So…there's a friend of mine coming to the party. He's not from Penn Washington, he's three years older than you, and his name is Chandler. He said that he'd be willing to help you study for the bar if you were interested."

I shoot my father a look of bewilderment.

"Has it come to this? My dad is fixing me up on dates now."

"Not at all, Juliette. This is not a date. The bar is not an easy exam. I think that you may be taking it too lightly. Chandler has spent the last two years helping other law students pass it. He's got a way with remembering terms, laws, and statutes that's remarkable."

"Can he show me how to get a photographic memory?" I jest. "Because that's the only way I'm going to remember half of the information that I need to pass this thing."

"You were never a good test taker."

"Thanks a lot, dad."

"I'm just saying. We all have our strengths and weaknesses. Just because you have to work harder at passing the examination doesn't make you any less intelligent or incapable. You will be an amazing lawyer. You're a Hill after all."

"That's true, I am," I say in agreement–ready to leave the backyard and this conversation in the worst way. I was completely over it before it even began. It's all anyone wants to talk to me about.

The bar.

The bar.

The bar.

"I'll introduce you two at the party," he says while clumsily climbing down the ladder. "His name is Chandler Branson."

There was no use in objecting. Resistance is futile when it comes to my parents' determination to make me a lawyer. One is a social climber (mom) and the other a cutthroat lawyer and judge (dad) who only cares about work and the family legacy.

"All right, dad. I'll meet him to see if there's anything he can do to help my fried brain absorb information better. Your sons were certainly no help. It was like teaching me to ride a bike all over again. Complete failure."

Almost every member of my family who's a lawyer has already tried to help me study for the bar. Seeing that I've already failed it once, my father is resorting to turning to strangers now. Strangers that he considers are dating material as well.

Truly pitiful.

Those *he's not from Penn Washington* and *he's three years older than you* comments that my father made were to let me know that Chandler is a viable candidate for marriage. My parents are definitely old school in some respects. While they want me to carve out my own career in law, they've also made it crystal clear that they expect me to get married and give them a bunch of grandkids sooner rather than later.

They want a whole lot don't they?

After my father finishes climbing down from the ladder, I interlock my arm with his and we walk back into the house where my mom is sorting through stemware.

"Are the lights up?" she asks my father in a curt manner. It's all business when she's planning this party.

"Yes, dear."

"Has it started snowing yet?"

"No, dear. I think the meteorologists just needed something to talk about today. I don't think there's any snow coming."

Yet I don't agree.

A storm or something akin to one is definitely coming.

I can feel it.

JOSEPH

I give myself a good long look in the mirror as I tighten the slipknot of my favorite silk tie. For the first time in my life, I'm dressed in a thousand dollar Ralph Lauren suit and a pair of Italian made shoes, and while I really like how I look in them–I love even more how I feel in them.

Like a million fucking bucks.

"Let's go, Joseph."

"Yep, I'm ready."

I've spent the better part of the last five years establishing myself as the number one problem solver for my employer, Lawyer Jack Mills. I started working for his firm as an assistant in the mailroom when Jack noticed my work ethic and my desire to move up in the company.

I remember him taking a long look at my hands, specifically my knuckles (which were worn and swollen from kicking some guy's ass at a bar the previous night) and asked me if I wanted a job outside of the mailroom.

My supervisor had held his position for over thirteen years, and while that was a good gig for a guy like him, there was no way that I wanted to end up permanently delivering mail to lawyers for the rest of my life.

"We'll see how you handle yourself." I remember Jack saying. "And if you solve my problem, you'll never have to work in the mailroom again."

I knew as soon as the words flew out of his mouth that this was the opportunity that I'd been waiting for. This was my ticket out of delivering manilla envelopes all day and into Jack's world of corporate law with real businessmen. While I wasn't a lawyer, and didn't have the smarts, the money, nor the desire to become one—I wanted a better life. That I knew for sure. And Jack was my ticket there.

So he hired me to make a paternity suit go away for a client who had always been a huge headache for him. He was a local newscaster. A big deal in

Philadelphia. He'd been an anchor on the local news for most of my life, and he'd gotten a woman pregnant outside of his marriage.

She worked as a receptionist at the station, and made it clear that she would tell anyone who would listen that she was pregnant with his child if he didn't leave his wife. Well, that was never going to happen, and pretty soon she realized it, so she hired a lawyer. She was going to file a lawsuit against him and sue him publicly for all types of shit including child support. It was my job to change her mind about that.

I didn't mind the job, but I don't hurt women—especially pregnant ones, so I knew I'd have to be creative about it. It was my first job, my first "fix" for Jack, and I needed to make sure that it was done just right. No mess.

I decided to follow her for a couple of days, observing her patterns, watching what stores she frequented, the company that she kept—and then I figured it out. Her Achilles heel was what it is for most of us—family.

She had a younger brother who apparently was the apple of her entire family's eye. A golden child. The two of us were around the same age, but he was in medical school, and planning on being a specialized surgeon. I knew that hurting him just a little bit would scare her more than anything.

He made it easy though. He was a pompous, arrogant, know-it-all who needed a lesson in basic manners. I overheard him as he rudely rushed an older woman who in his opinion was taking too long to check out of the supermarket.

She was couponing, probably on a fixed budget, and she was somebody's damn mama. He didn't need to talk to her like that. It was a real bitch move, him embarrassing that sweet old lady in the market that day, and it rubbed me completely the wrong way. So I took a lot of pleasure in beating his ass right in front of his pregnant sister.

The receptionist was my first "fix" for Jack, and I'll always remember her. She was tough as hell, and held out until the bitter end. I almost had to snap a few of those kid's fingers, but at the very last minute she acquiesced. A med student can't be a surgeon with messed up hands.

So she agreed to recant her public statement about the client's cheating, drop the paternity case, and to accept a monthly stipend to keep her mouth zipped. All for the beautifully dirt cheap settlement price of nine-hundred dollars a month.

No one had ever been able to negotiate that type

of very one-sided deal for their clients before, and Jack's popularity as a problem solver at the firm quickly began to grow. With his meteoric rise in the firm came my rise as well and because of that one opportunity, I will never have to see the inside of a mailroom again.

"Where exactly are we going?" I ask my boss.

"This is my first time getting an invite to this holiday party, so let me warn you now, they must want something, and most likely it's to hire me aka you to fix something for them."

"I thought I was your best kept secret."

"Not from them."

"Who's them?"

"The Hill Family. Family full of lawyers who think they're way more important than they really are, but even I admit that they are well connected in the tri-state area. So I have to play the game. Act like I give a shit about this party and them when I don't."

"Understood."

When we arrive in front of the large colonial home, in the suburb of Penn Washington of all places, I can't believe my luck.

What are the fucking chances?

It's *her* house.

Juliette.

The beautiful teenaged girl, who I fell for in one fleeting afternoon, lived here years ago. I wonder if she still lives here now?

I was meeting a friend who worked in the cafeteria at her high school. He owed me four hundred dollars for covering his rent the month before, and I was coming to collect. Our meeting was brief. He gave me my money and I was on my way back to my car, when I overheard a conversation between Juliette and a guy that I could only assume was her boyfriend.

Where I'm from, you don't talk to girls like that unless you have a real good reason. We don't even treat our neighborhood sluts the way that he treated Juliette that day. He let his friends watch them have sex and it was her first time?

I didn't even know her, but I was immediately proud of the way that she was standing up to him, calling him on his shit, and doing it in front of half the damn student body. But then he took it too far. Saying out loud, to anyone who would listen, that beautiful girl gave him a disease?

That girl?

The girl who probably has fairies and butterflies shooting out of her asshole because she's so sweet?

There was no way in hell.

And then when she ran away, tears streaming down her face, something in me snapped.

So I kicked his ass.

And I did it willingly and joyfully.

I also dared every one of those soft ass friends of his to say one word about it, or I promised that I would come back for each and every one of them, every single day, until I had dealt with the entire fucking team.

I meant that shit.

And I think they took me for my word.

No one did a thing about it.

This girl had the power to make me do things that I'd never done before. I'd never fought over a girl. I never met one that inspired such a reaction out of me. The feeling was new to me–a foreign and almost frightening experience. Yet it was one of the most memorable afternoons of my life.

I drove Juliette home and we talked about all kinds of things that I didn't normally talk about with anyone: politics, television, the internet, cell phones, music. I revealed so much to her during that long ride home. Things that I'd never shared with anyone.

I fell hard for her that day, but I'm the first to admit that my dick was doing all the thinking–not my brain. Because as soon as I pulled up in front of that pristine, colonial, five-bedroom house–the one that we're in front of right now.

It hit me.

We were from two completely different worlds.

This would never work.

I could never be who she needed. Who she deserved.

So I dropped her off, and promised that I would call, but I never did and the plan was that I never would.

Yet here we fucking are.

I'm dressed in a body skimming red cocktail gown that drops dangerously low in the back with red heels. I promised my mother that I would dress for the occasion, and honestly I don't mind getting dolled up for her holiday party. It's the only time of year that I actually wear something semiformal. Most of the time I'm in workout clothes (because I'm a gym rat) or jeans.

"You look amazing, darling," my father says.

"Thanks, daddy."

"Nice lipstick," my mother comments. "Where'd you get that shade?"

"It's by MAC."

"Never heard of them."

"You have to walk away from the Estee Lauder

counter once in a while and check out some other product lines," I snicker. "Everyone wears MAC now."

"Can you help me go over a few things with the caterer, Juliette? They're short on staff at the last minute, so I'm afraid we're going to have to help them out a little tonight. You're so good at getting the little details of this event right every time."

"Sure, mom. It's fun. I'll do it."

"I'm so relived that the weather held up. We should get a good turnout."

"You always get a good turnout."

"Your father mentioned that Chandler was coming tonight?"

"You know him too?"

Surprise. Surprise.

"He helped Sally's son pass the bar."

"Mom, I think you should know that I'm having second thoughts about the whole law thing."

"What do you mean, Juliette?" she asks as she counts the number of wine glasses and champagne flutes that are clean. "Who has second thoughts about being a lawyer when they're finished the hard part?"

"I'm thinking that law school and passing the bar

were difficult for me, because it's not really what I'm supposed to be doing."

"Don't be ridiculous. It's what we do."

"You don't do it."

She stops rinsing out flutes and looks up at me.

"Your grandfather didn't believe in handouts as he put it. He wouldn't give your father a dime to pay for his education. So I worked as a secretary to put your dad through law school, so that I'd have the luxury of staying at home and raising my family when the time came," she states defensively.

"I know the story, mom. I'm just saying that you weren't a lawyer and you're just fine. You're happy and fulfilled."

"You don't think you could have figured that out six years ago? What about all of your schooling? All of the money we paid? Are you just going to throw it all away?"

She's right.

It would be crazy to start all over again.

"Maybe Chandler can give you some advice on getting back on track or finding a type of law that you'd like to practice. You don't have to work in the courts like your brothers or your father. Maybe you just have to find your niche."

My father peeps his head in the door.

"Chandler's here."

Right on cue.

"Go out there with an open mind, Juliette. He's a nice boy."

Chandler is a nice guy. Handsome, smart and friendly. Definitely a well raised man. If he has one flaw it seems to be that he's a little intimidated by my family, specifically my oldest brothers, but that's ok. I'm not trying to marry the guy. I just need a little help passing the bar. I could at least try to pass the thing, before I make any final decisions about my law career.

Then the ground shifts.

I'm talking to him about my law school escapades and forcing myself to laugh at one of his corny "law jokes" when I see the last person on earth I'd expect to ever see again walk through my front door.

It's him.

It's Joseph.

He's dressed in a suit that fits him like a glove, and he walks through the threshold of my house side by side with a man that I've seen before. Both of them strutting in like they own the place.

"Your honor," the man says to my father.

"Jack."

Oh, now I know who he is. He's the infamous

Jack Mills. I've heard my brothers mention him and his practice before.

"This is the guy I was telling you about, Mr. Hill. This is Joseph."

"Nice to meet you, Joe. I've heard a lot of good things about you."

"Likewise."

Wow, he looks incredible. While he is pretty much the same height as he was years ago (tall as hell), his body has filled out in almost every single place you can think of.

His biceps, shoulders, and thighs are all larger and more defined than I remember. His hair is neatly coiffed but his eyes…they are still dark and dangerous and fixated directly on me.

The oxygen in the room seems to evaporate.

I can't breathe.

What do I say to this man?

What do I say to someone who makes me feel seventeen again? The person who made me feel so beautiful on my darkest day, but then disappeared like a puff of smoke.

You say nothing, Juliette.

You go reheat the platter of crab puffs in the kitchen and forget about him.

"Excuse me, Chandler. I need to check on something for dinner."

"Of course."

I make a beeline for my bedroom instead, shut the door, and start hyperventilating. My first thought is to call Karen, because she knows all about Joseph. I had to tell her, because it was all anyone talked about for weeks when I got back to school.

Especially because every football player in school avoided eye contact with me. It was like having an invisible cloak of protection during my last days in that building. They were scared shitless of Joseph.

Unfortunately though, those carefree days of us sharing each other's secrets are long gone. After graduation we fell out of touch. Karen enrolled in a conservatory program in New York for the violin, and I stayed in Pennsylvania and attended Villanova University for undergrad.

I guess I'm going to have to work through this chance meeting on my own doing what I do best—avoidance.

Of course I may be panicking for nothing and giving myself way too much credit. It was six years ago. What if he doesn't remember me at all?

I hear a firm rap on my bedroom door, but I sit frozen on the edge of my bed. My gut is telling me that it's him.

He knocks again. This time the knock is firmer.

"Juliette, open the door."

Holy shit, it's him. He does remember.

"Hi," is all I say as I answer the door.

He lazily rakes his eyes up and down the length of my body. Settling them for a moment on my hips, then the curve of my waist, and then back to my face.

"Hi, can I come in?"

"Uh, sure."

He enters my room and closes the door behind him.

"You look amazing."

I look away and smile.

"Thank you."

"Are you a lawyer now?" he asks.

"Not yet, I still have to take the bar examination."

"I knew you'd do big things."

"And what about you? What do you do that you've been invited to my parents' Christmas party?"

"I work for Jack Mills."

"Are you a lawyer too?"

"Not even close."

"Oh."

He takes a few steps closer and grabs both of my wrists.

"I'm sorry about how I left things, Juliette."

"Left things?" I feign ignorance while pulling my arms gently out of his grasp.

He lifts my chin with his hand, so that my eyes meet his.

"I'm usually a man of my word, and I said that I would call, but I didn't. There were reasons for that, but I was wrong and I'm sorry."

"Oh, that? Don't worry about it. It was a lifetime ago, and I wasn't actually expecting you to call."

I'm pretending right now. I actually waited

months (until the day I left for Villanova) for Joseph to call.

I even got desperate enough to ask a few kids like study hall guy what they knew about him, but my research was for naught. A lot of people heard of him but didn't know anything concrete about him. No phone number. No address. Nothing.

"Liar."

"What?"

"It's obvious when you're lying. You have a *tell*. You bite the inside corner of your lip."

"I do not," I protest.

"Most people have a tell. That's kind of my forte. Reading people's energy."

"Well, you're not that good at it."

He snickers.

"If you're angry with me, Juliette, just tell me. I'm a big boy. I can take it."

"I was never angry."

I don't know how I missed it six years ago, but I notice that Joseph has a pretty prominent cleft chin. I can't keep my eyes off of it. Off of him.

He looks twenty times better than my late night fantasies could ever have conjured up. Confidence, dominance, and desire rolls off of him in waves.

"That's even worse." His voice drops a few

octaves. "That means I didn't leave enough of an impression."

My mother suddenly knocks on the door.

"Juliette, are you all right in there?"

"Yes, Mom," I respond nervously. I'm almost twenty-five years old, but the same house rules still apply whether I'm twelve or twenty-five. No boys (or grown men) in my bedroom other than my brothers and my father.

"Chandler is looking lonely out here." She imagines herself whispering through the door. "Get back out here."

"Coming, Mom."

Joseph has an icy look on his face and his posture stiffens.

"Who's Chandler?"

"Just a guy."

"And why would you care that he's lonely?"

"I don't."

"Is he your date tonight?"

"I'm not dating."

His face quickly softens.

"You're not?"

"No."

"You sure?"

Then Joseph slides one of his hands in the base of

my scalp pulling me towards him with firm assurance. My thong instantly become moist with desire in response.

"I asked if you were sure, Juliette."

Before I can answer him, he slides his tongue inside of my mouth and my body immediately hums with approval and aches with desire. It's the most intimate kiss I've ever shared with any man.

In fact it was actually less of a kiss and more of a claiming. In just this moment, after all of these years, Joseph has claimed me. I pray he doesn't disappear on me again. It might just wreck me.

"I'm sure," I say in between heavy panting.

"Keep your eyes on mine when you talk to me, Juliette. I want to search them for truth, for lies, and for everything in between. I have never forgotten you. Not for one single second. And now that destiny has brought us together again, I plan on us getting to know each other a lot better."

He slides a hand inside of the slit of my dress and gently in between my legs.

"For a very long time."

"Joseph," I moan.

"Let me make sure you leave this room with a smile on your face. You're going to need it when you go back out there and give poor Chandler the brush off."

"But I have to go out there and talk to him because–"

"I don't share, Juliette."

Two of Joseph's thick fingers slide under the stain fabric of my panties and in between my folds. I close my eyes in pure rapture.

I've never been given this much pleasure before, mostly because after the debacle of my first sexual experience in high school, I shied away from anything physical with guys I was dating.

Once it got to that point, I would find a way to bow out. But this right here and right now feels absolutely perfect.

"Eyes on me, Juliette."

I stare directly into Joseph's bottomless pupils as he continues to stroke my clit.

"I'm going to make you come with my hand, and then I'm going to clean you up with my tongue, and then you're going to go out there and give Chandler the brush off."

Every single word he just said turned me on so hard that I could come right now.

"Are we in agreement?" he asks.

"Yes."

"Wrap your arms around my neck and lean into me."

I silently follow instructions.

"I'm going to slide my fingers inside of you now, and I want you to fuck them."

I whimper in ecstasy and in a bit of embarrassment. His words are so dirty but such a turn on.

"That's good, baby," he croons as his fingers ram in and out of me.

"Shhh," I breathlessly warn. "No one can know that you're in here."

He laughs almost sinisterly.

"You're the one who's going to have to try hard to be quiet, Juliette."

His fingers pick up momentum and I find my hips meeting him thrust for thrust. I'm about to come. I don't want to. I want this to go on for forever, but he is working my body like he is fine tuning an underused instrument and getting it in pitch perfect condition.

I want to scream as I orgasm, but realizing all the people who are on the other side of that door, I decide instead to muffle my release into the lapel of his suit jacket.

"That's it, baby. Come for me." He continues to coax my orgasm to completion.

Then he drops to his knees and orders me lift my dress.

"Lift your dress to your waist, hold it high, and be quiet for me a little longer while I clean you up."

When Joseph's warm mouth descends upon my pussy, it's like an out of body experience. I don't know how he thinks I'm supposed to stay still and not say a word like this. Or maybe that's the point? To torture me in my own damn house.

He holds me still with his hands on my ass, and talks to me in between laps of his tongue.

"This is the sweetest pussy I've ever had."

Another lick.

"I want to own this."

A gentle suck.

"Can you come for me again, baby?"

As he continues to clean my release with his mouth, I can feel another orgasm beginning to wind and coil inside of me.

"Joseph," I mutter in blissful misery. "I think–"

"Yeah," he growls. "I definitely think you're ready."

At this point I can't talk.

I can barely think straight.

All I feel is pleasure and adoration of this man on his knees for me.

"Come for me, Juliette. Right the fuck now."

I open my mouth to scream but nothing comes out. Tiny little explosions pop like popcorn inside of my head and behind my tautly shut eyelids as I come harder than imaginable. In my childhood bedroom. By a man who has absolutely ruined me for any other.

I belong to Joseph now.

There is no turning back.

I grin to myself as I take a swig of my bourbon neat, because all I can still taste is Juliette on my tongue. The taste is even sweeter, because I'm savoring it while sitting in the private home office of her father–the Honorable Judge Hill with Jack and her two brothers.

Jack was right. This was not a social invitation. We were invited to the judge's annual holiday party for a reason. His two sons work in a private legal practice and want to hire Jack's firm to handle several fixes for them that are sensitive in nature or in other words–illegal.

It's obvious that they wanted me to tag along, because they are fully aware that Jack doesn't do any of the dirty work. I do. And they want to see for themselves what their big fat check is going to get them.

I'm not sure where Juliette gets her beautiful spirit from, because the rest of the family reminds me of everything I detest about privilege. They're arrogant, pretentious, pompous and act as if I should feel honored just to be sitting in their presence–especially the oldest brother.

It's clear that he thinks himself to be superior to me in intelligence, wealth and class. The truth is that he might just be, but I don't give a rat's ass. I'll buy my way into their world and piss on them as I climb my way up.

"So if my boys hire you, Jack, you'll take care of them right?"

"I'm sure you've asked around. My firm specializes in neat and tidy. Nothing will blow back on them."

"We'll be dealing directly with you though, right Jack?" the obnoxious one asks as he stares at me. Even in my designer suit and shoes, I'm not fooling them one iota. They know I'm from the streets, it's in my DNA, and they don't like it one bit.

"The firm can accommodate whatever communication style you feel is most beneficial."

"Is there a problem dealing with me?" I ask having enough of his passive aggressive ass.

The energy in the room grows tense.

"I've heard things about you over the years, Masterson. You're not new to me," he says in an almost accusatory way.

"I'm assuming that's why you want to hire me."

"We're hiring Jack, not you."

"For a fix like this, Joseph and I are a packaged deal," Jack chimes in. "I hope that's not going to be a problem."

"No problem," Juliette's father says wanting to ease the tension in the room. He gives his son a cursory glare. "We're definitely moving forward. The boys need their issue resolved. However you both make that happen is none of our concern."

There's a small knock on the door and then it opens without the person waiting for permission to enter.

It's Juliette.

I was in between her legs just thirty minutes ago, but looking at her now, an absolute temptress in red, makes my dick weep and long to be inside of her.

I already know that when it happens between us, when she allows me to totally claim her body and soul, it will be life changing for the both of us.

Our chemistry cannot be denied.

She is mine.

The moment Juliette notices me sitting across from her family, her expression gives our connection immediately away. It's obvious to anyone with half of a brain that we know each other.

"Do you know my sister?" the younger brother asks in a voice full of disbelief while the rest of the room stares down my throat.

"I do."

"Juliette?" Her father defers to her to explain.

"I met Joseph several years ago, so yes, he and I are acquainted."

"Where on earth—"

Her brother interrupts. "Several years ago?"

"Yes, in high school," she further explains.

"Oh, now that I've seen you and my sister in the same room, I'm wondering. Are you the mysterious stranger from the hood who beat up the ball player on Franklin's campus in broad daylight?"

"What are you talking about?" Judge Hill chimes back in. "What does that have to do with Juliette?"

"I am *that* kid from the hood," I say matter of factly. "And that ball player everybody was so worried about disrespected your sister."

I don't want to get in details about that day,

because I have no idea what Juliette has shared with her family, but I'm not going to allow her brother to drag my name in this like I did something wrong. I did everything right that day. That asshole deserved an ass whipping.

"You're volatile and unpredictable," he says.

"That was also a long time ago. I would handle things today with a level of maturity that I didn't have back then."

Nah, I'm lying. I'd still kick his ass.

"Can I speak with you for a moment, Jules?"

The brother summons Juliette, exits the room with her, and closes the door behind them. I can only imagine what he's saying to her, but right now I have to deal with the rest of the people in the room.

"So, Joe–"

"Please call me Joseph, Mr. Hill. Very few people are permitted to call me Joe."

Juliette's father adjusts himself uncomfortably in his chair. I assume that not many people talk to him so directly.

"Joseph then...I'll just be blunt about this. What business do you have with my daughter?"

"No *business* at all–we're friends."

"Friends?"

"Yes."

Jack looks at me like as though he'd wish we were having a conversation about anything other than Hill's daughter, but he doesn't say a word. He may be my employer, but we share a mutual respect for each other.

"I appreciate whatever you did for her when she was in high school, Joseph, but I'd rather you two not remain…so friendly."

"Why is that, Mr. Hill? I have nothing but great respect and admiration for your daughter."

"I'm just not comfortable mixing business and pleasure. It's a conflict of interest."

"If we're really going to be technical about this–" I start to say until Jack clears his throat to interrupt me. It's his classic signal for me to shut up, but I'm not listening this time.

This time I have Juliette all over and inside of my mouth, which has awakened a hunger in me that I didn't know existed.

I don't deserve her but fuck it.

She's worth it.

She is worth fighting for.

"If we're going to be technical about this, you shouldn't even be in this room, Mr. Hill. You're a judge, not just a father. Your relationship with your boys and your job on the bench are what's in direct conflict here not whatever friendship I may or may not have with your daughter."

The old man stands up.

"She is *my* only daughter."

I nod in recognition and in respect.

"I understand that."

"So let's keep things strictly professional. That's all I'm asking."

"I am, Mr. Hill." I take a swallow of my drink and stare him down to challenge his resolve. "I will take care of your sons' dilemma at work, I will be a good friend to your daughter, and never the twain shall meet."

Juliette's father turns beet red. Probably not a good way to get on my future father-in-law's good side (because rest assured I will be marrying Juliette Hill one day), but he needs to know.

They all need to know.

I will not be talked down to or talked at. I am motherfucking Joseph Masterson, and I demand and deserve the respect of everyone in the room.

"We need to speak to Jack alone now," brother number two says to me.

"No problem, it's been a pleasure. I look forward to working with you."

When I exit the office, I immediately scan the

room, looking for Juliette. I find her sitting in an area they call the "great room" on one of the many love seats in this house, sandwiched in between a man who looks exactly like her (must be the 3rd youngest brother) and a man whom I can only assume is the infamous Chandler. He's young, dressed like a lawyer, and is looking at Juliette like she's a snack.

I walk directly up on them and extend my hand forward.

"Are you ready to finish giving me that tour, Juliette?" I ask her.

"A tour?"

"I'd love to see some of the *other* rooms in your house."

My girl stands but her face turns a beautiful shade of dusky pink when she does.

"Jules," her brother warns.

Oh, this one hates me too?

Perfect.

"Juliette?" My hand is still extended.

I want her to grab it.

Choose me, Juliette.

Trust me, baby.

"Jules, this is a bad idea," the brother says.

When Juliette grabs my hand and slides her every

one of her slender fingers in between mine, my entire body finally relaxes and exhales.

This is *her* claiming.

She is mine and I am hers.

I lean over and whisper in her ear, "Thank you, baby."

She turns her head and kisses me swiftly on the lips.

"Let's go look at the lights my father hung outside."

"Whatever you want."

And that's my promise to her.

Whatever she wants.

Whenever she wants it.

However she likes it.

I'm going to fight like hell for the rest of our lives to give her whatever she wants and to make sure that I'm worthy of a woman like Juliette. I'm going to be a good provider, a strong leader, a giving lover, and a man of my word.

I will never let her down again.

Why?

Because she's fucking worth it.

Ready for your next antihero? Get ready for the next story in the spinoff series about The King Brothers. Read Jade & Camden King's super HOT and twisted story in **CLAIMED.**

TAP TO DOWNLOAD THE BOOK INSTANTLY

Continue reading for excerpt…

The Harbor Hotel
Baltimore, Maryland
Three Months Ago

CAMDEN

I'm not a big talker.

I keep to myself.

If someone needs to make a lot of noise, I let my brother Cutter handle that. Cutter often describes me as the silent and deadly type. That may be a somewhat accurate characterization of me, but I like to think of myself as careful instead.

A watcher.

Someone who calculates risk before taking it.

Someone who observes a situation long and hard before striking. But when I finally do make the decision to act, I don't fuck around. I handle my business. Which is what brings me here standing in front of the five-star Harbor Hotel of Baltimore, Maryland.

I've run a million scenarios in my head.

I've calculated the risk.

And I think it's fucking worth it.

Tonight … I'm taking what's mine.

I've been patient long enough.

The Harbor Hotel
Baltimore, Maryland
Three Months Ago

I'M IN THE BATHROOM, in my birthday suit, contemplating the day I've just had. As I sip on my second large cocktail consisting of Grey Goose vodka and pineapple juice over ice, I finish wiping off the remnants of my so-called waterproof mascara, and start running the tub when I hear a knock at my hotel room door.

I'm feeling no pain, but the knock is loud enough

that I hear it over my old school nineties jams streaming through an app on my phone. I don't think anything of the interruption, though, because I'm expecting an overpriced Cobb salad and an iced tea from room service. So I wrap the oversized bath sheet around my nude body, run to the door, crack it open to let the server in, and immediately turn back to attend to my tub full of water.

"You can just leave the platter on the bed," I call out. Running back to the bubbles and cocktail waiting for me. But it isn't anyone from room service. It's a greeting from a deep, rolling, familiar voice that makes my stomach flip and flutter instead.

"Where are you running off to, itty bitty?"

I whip my head around in shock. Strands of my hair flying in my mouth. Only one person calls me that particular nickname, and he has no business being here.

"What the hell?!" The words tumble out of my mouth.

"Come again?"

The *voice* doesn't like it when I curse at him. Never mind the fact that he has a foul mouth too. Never mind the fact that he is here invading *my* space, not the other way around, so in my opinion a couple of curse words are definitely called for.

"Let me speak clearer for you then." I make sure to enunciate all my consonants and vowels. Especially the bad ones. "What the *hell* are you doing in my hotel room? No wait, what the *fuck* are you doing in Maryland, period?"

"Handling some business, and watch your fucking mouth."

My boss Camden King, deliciously dressed in all black, steps completely into my room, lets the door click shut, and carefully drops his signature black leather backpack on the floor. As soon as I hear the thump of his bag hitting the carpeted entryway, the room suddenly becomes several square feet smaller.

I can barely breathe.

His cocky dominance takes up so much oxygen, and there's a seriousness etched across his beautifully chiseled face that frightens and fascinates me at the same time.

"What business?" I ask with a faux confidence. Not even realizing that I am walking backwards towards the wall as he moves silently forward like the predator that he is quickly revealing himself to be.

I stop moving when I can't any longer, my back finally against the wall, white knuckling the corners of my towel, making sure that it stays closed.

Because if it slips even just a little, I think I will end up slipping.

Slipping right on top of his enormous dick.

I hate to admit it to myself, but *doing* Camden King has been a reoccurring theme in many of my dreams lately. Dreams I hoped would cease very soon, because they are a pain in my ass and a strain on my vibrator. Not to mention that I couldn't or wouldn't ever make the decision to *actually* fuck my boss.

Only in my dreams.

Or so I keep telling myself.

The two of us stare at each other for a moment in uneasy silence. We don't really need words at the moment, because the fact that he is here speaks volumes. Camden doesn't travel much outside of the Philadelphia area. Not unless it's absolutely required for a job, and being in Baltimore was certainly not a job requirement. We don't have any clients in the area, and we both are actually supposed to be somewhere else tonight.

The beauty of my relationship with my employers: Camden, Cutter and Roman has always been that it's a simple and straight forward relationship. I work for them. They pay me. I take care of them. They protect me. But we give each other a wide berth when it comes to our private lives. They have their women. Lots of women. And I've had my dalliances too, but no one interferes in each other's lives.

At least not until today.

"What are you doing in this hotel, Jade?" he asks while closing the gap between us even more. "Why aren't you home attending the fundraiser?"

There was an important autism fundraising event hosted by Roman's stepmother that we both were supposed to attend. I was planning all week to be there, but decided at the last minute to come here instead. I didn't tell anyone where I was going, because there would have been too many questions. Questions I wasn't ready to answer.

"Why aren't *you* there?" I counter.

"I asked first," he says while flashing that very wicked smile of his.

"What business is it of yours?"

"Last time I checked you are my business." He takes a long pause for effect then finishes his thought. "You work for me, remember?"

"Well if you want to get technical about things, Roman is the one who hired me."

"I think you're very confused." Camden practically growls in my face.

At this point, we are standing so close to each other that I feel drenched in his scent. All of the domineering men I work for have a signature aroma, but Camden always smells the best. Earthy and natural. Like he sweats sandalwood and leather. The scent is utterly intoxicating and must be permanently etched in my olfactory senses, because sometimes I wake up in the morning and swear that I can actually smell him in my apartment. Which is completely impossible, because Camden has never been inside of my place, and Lord knows that I'm trying to keep it that way.

"You answer to three men. Roman, me, and my brother. Of course tonight you have the distinct pleasure of only having to answer to me," he says while running the backs of his fingers gingerly down the side of my face. The unexpected touch of his calloused knuckles almost takes my breath away. *What is he doing?*

"Listen, Camden—"

"No, you listen."

He's so close that his lips are actually touching mine as he continues to speak. His eyes almost dancing. "I tracked you, I followed you, and I'm not leaving until I get what I came for."

He firmly grabs me around my waist with one

hand, and places his other on the hand that is holding my towel in place.

"What did you—"

He cuts off my idiotic question with his mouth, and kisses me like he was trying to teach me a lesson. A lesson on how to fuck someone's mouth properly. A lesson on how to shut a woman up in the most pleasurable way possible. A lesson on never questioning why Camden does anything he does. It would be pointless. Especially if he was going to do shit like this to stop me.

I haven't allowed myself to completely let go though. I'm still highly strung like a tightly wound clock, because I haven't been kissed like this since … well I've never been kissed like this. I've only had one serious relationship in my life, which was a complete disaster from start to finish, and then a string of meaningless fucks afterwards.

I never kiss them.

It's one of my rules.

A rule I seem to have completely thrown to the wayside as Camden's tongue expertly and languidly explores mine. Soft, tender, exploratory strokes of his tongue that are loosening me up with each swipe. His skills are so amazing that they make me wonder just how good it would feel if he used them on other areas of my body.

Probably would be life changing.

There's no way I can let things get to that point though, because that would be damn near close to breaking my *never going to fuck my boss* rule. Unfortunately Camden's expert command of my mouth and my inability to respond appropriately because of it starts to shake my resolve.

I release the taut hold I had on my towel. Then he lifts his hand away from mine and slides it in my hair at the nape of my neck.

Cradling the back and side of my head.

Stroking his thumb gently near the corner of my mouth.

Pulling me farther into him.

Deepening our kiss.

And ratcheting up the heat factor.

I completely let go of the towel. It feels stupid to keep holding onto it in the middle of us passionately making out, because that is indeed what we are doing, even though my hands are still in between us. Serving as the last remaining barrier between the two of us making full bodily contact.

I can't place my arms around his neck like I want to,

because Camden is so much taller than me, so I slide them around his waist instead. Decision made. If this is going to happen, then it's going to happen. Maybe it was meant to be. There's no one here to interrupt us. There's no one to talk me out of it. There's just me and him. No one will have to know. It could be a one time thing. Another meaningless fuck. It would have to be.

He's my boss and someone I've known for a long time, and because of those two things, he knows entirely too much about me, and I know quite a bit about him as well. Things that would make going beyond one night complicated and awkward. So yeah, it could never be more than one night in this hotel room for both of our sakes.

Camden abruptly pulls away from the kiss and glares at me almost angrily. As if he's upset that he's just kissed me, or something. *Me too, buddy*, I think to myself. I never thought I would be kissing Camden King naked in a hotel room.

Honestly, I have no idea what he's thinking. Which is one of the things that drives me absolutely nuts about Camden. I can't read his facial expressions or lack thereof for shit. Which makes handling him that much more of a challenge. It's always been like that, and oddly enough, one of the things that draws me to him.

"What?" I ask open-mouthed.

He slowly rakes his eyes up and down my nude body before asking the craziest question.

"Are you fucking someone here?"

"What?!"

"Did I stutter? I asked you if you're fucking someone."

"What does that matter?"

"Not the right answer, Jade."

"Don't make this more difficult."

"Don't make *what* more difficult?"

"Whatever I think is about to happen in this room."

"Nothing is going to happen in this room until you tell me if you're fucking someone or not."

"Are you actually trying to throw down an ulti-matum? Let's not forget that I didn't invite you here. You barged your way in here. I could care less whether anything happens between us tonight or not."

"Your pussy begs to differ."

"You don't know shit about what's in between my legs, and you never will."

I bend down to pick up my towel, suddenly very self-conscious about my lack of clothing.

"Anyone who stepped inside of this room right

now would know. You can smell it. It's wet. It's weeping. It's hungry. And I made it that way."

For just a moment his gifted kissing technique made me forget what an arrogant prick Camden King can be, and the reason why I in fact have rules in place to begin with.

"Get out," I order firmly.

"I'm not going any motherfucking where," he growls.

"I don't want you here. Get out—"

He cuts my words off again, but this time with one of his hands wrapped around my throat and the other shoved between my legs. I inadvertently drop the towel again, and immediately feel a warm gush between my legs as he slides his fingers back and forth between my folds.

Assertively and expertly.

My knees would have buckled if it weren't for the fact that he was firmly holding me against the wall by my neck. I am so turned on by his passionate manhandling of me, I can't think straight and the yeses seem to keep flying out of my mouth.

"Do you like how this feels, Jade?"

"Yes," I moan like the weakling the vodka has made me.

"Do you want me to keep doing this until you come on my hand?"

Dammit, he's dirty too.

"Yes," I exhale in defeat.

"So are you going to be a good girl and answer my question?" His deep voice rumbles closely beside my ear as he continues to stroke me between my legs.

"Yes," I gasp in pleasure.

"Yes you *are* fucking someone here?"

His hand stops moving.

"No," I puff out in frustration. Sick of the twenty questions. "The only person I'm fucking is you in about three seconds in this hotel room."

"Good fucking answer, itty bitty."

I'M TOTALLY MIND FUCKED. The second after I give Camden the answer he wants to hear his hands instantly drop down and away from me. I can't believe how my body immediately misses his confident grasp, the slight pressure around my neck, and the way he was stroking me. Somehow without prior knowledge, this big pain in my ass knows exactly what my body likes and what it needs, and God help me, but I'm desperately craving more.

"Pick up the towel you dropped and spread it on the bed. I don't care how nice of a hotel this is, hotel bed spreads are gross."

I do what he asks as he starts taking off his jacket, but there is something about touching the towel again that triggers my memory. The water.

"Shit!" I scream as I take off flying towards the bathroom. "I left the tub running."

Sure enough there is the beginning of a major flood in the beautiful marbled bathroom of my five-star hotel room. Well more than just the beginnings. The floor is damn near completely covered in water, and I know I'll have to pay a mint if I don't quickly figure out a way to sop it all up.

While I'm wading my feet in flood water, wondering what the heck I am going to do, Camden runs out into the hallway, locates a housekeeping cart, and swipes a stack of towels. Next thing I know, we both are on all fours, mopping up water with white fluffy towels, when room service knocks. I'm actually still naked as a jaybird, so Camden does the honor of answering the door.

"It better be fucking room service for one," he

says in an accusatory tone. Still obviously suspicious that I am in Baltimore to meet a man.

"Oh be quiet and get the door," I fuss back.

I hear Camden answer the door, mumble a few words, then close it; but when he never comes back into the bathroom, I get a little nervous. After finishing up wiping the last of the water, I go back out into the suite's main area to see what he's up to, and find that he has made himself quite comfortable.

The lights have been dimmed, the bedspread taken off, and the sheets of the bed are pulled down. He's taken off his black motorcycle boots, his shirt, and leather jacket. And all he is wearing are his black cargo pants, a leather cuff on his wrist, and a sexy smirk across his face.

I should be annoyed. He's being so ridiculously presumptuous. I mean have I ever given him reason to think that I'd be down for this? But it's difficult to be genuinely miffed about his impromptu visit when I'm practically drooling over the jerk right now.

He looks amazing.

Downright delicious.

I've always known that Camden takes care of himself. He eats well, works out, and I've definitely seen him without a shirt on over the years, but getting a full on view of his diamond cut six-pack in soft bedroom lighting, with that hungry look in his eyes is a whole other thing. I can't look away.

"Who was at the door?" I ask in a lame attempt to distract myself from the *real* distraction in the room.

"Room service and it looks like crap," he says as the metal lid clanks when he places it back over my salad. "We'll have to order from a better place later. I'm sure you'll have an appetite for something more than salad by then."

"What is going on with you Camden? Why are you doing this? Why are you here?"

Camden stares at me with a look of steely determination.

"Playing stupid doesn't suit you, Jade. You know exactly why I'm here. You've known for weeks. Maybe even months. There's something between us, and we're going to figure out what tonight. No more glares from across the room. No more ignoring me. No more smart-ass comments about who I'm fucking. No more silent treatment at meetings, because you don't know how to communicate when you're pissed."

My head is whirling. "I don't … I don't want this," I say.

Actually I've wanted this for months, but I've been fighting it. I think it would be a huge mistake that not just the two of us, but all four of us would never recover from.

"Get in the bed," he orders gruffly. "You lie entirely too much."

"Oh my freaking God, you've definitely lost touch with reality—"

"I think you're confused again." He shushes me. "When I tell you to get in the bed, I also mean for you to shut the fuck up."

"Like that will ever happen," I say. Not totally understanding that while my mouth chooses to oppose any and all orders he may give, my body delights in submitting to each and every one of his directives. In other words, I'm fucked.

"No?"

"No," I answer a lot less confidently.

"I've got the perfect way to shut you up. Get on the bed and scoot down. Head away from the headboard."

I follow directions but am shaking while I do.

My heart rapidly pounding.

My breath shortening.

Camden slowly unbuckles the thick leather belt he's wearing with his eyes completely on me. As he pulls the leather through his belt loops, I take a quick inhalation. Frightened that he plans on using the belt on me.

His eyebrow raises in curiosity. "You want the belt, Jade?"

I nod my head no as he chuckles in response. "Next time then."

I stay completely silent as he continues to unzip his pants, and lets them drop to the floor with a thud. My pupils are mono-focused on the growing bulge inside of his black fitted boxers. I think I may have just even licked my lips.

He waits for a moment.

Watching me.

Reading me.

I consider myself pretty tough, and it takes a lot to intimidate a girl like me, but he was doing a pretty good job of it.

When he finally slides his boxers down, I watch in delicious horror as his dick springs completely free. I say horror because I am four eleven, he's got to be at least six two, and his dick is big as shit. I mean I've always suspected it was huge, I've caught glimpses of it in it's flaccid state over the years, but seeing it live, erect, and in person makes what is about to go down between us seem *extra* real.

And fucking scary.

I'm worried.

If the glove doesn't fit, you must acquit, is the only nonsensical line I keep repeating to myself. What if it doesn't fit?

"Wait," is my one-word feeble attempt to stop him, and he does … after kicking his boxers across the room.

"I don't respond to the word *wait.* The only words you need to say are *stop* if you want this to end or *don't stop* if it feels good. You got me?"

I'm literally speechless as he continues on and climbs carefully onto the bed. Sitting above my head and against the headboard. His dick jutting out and bobbing angrily up and down over the top of my face.

"Hold onto my thighs and open your mouth," he directs.

Fuck, I swear to myself.

I'm so conflicted.

It never dawned on me that Camden would be so commanding in bed. This isn't exactly the way I pictured it in my fantasies. I may have to do what-ever he says at work, but in my dreams, I am the one in charge. Taking orders in bed is not something that I'm used to. Not with my one-night stands. With them I always take the lead and I always feel safe. But maybe letting go with someone I am very much attracted to, and someone I trust (to the degree that I can trust anyone) wouldn't be such a big deal. I've done worse things.

So I do what I'm told and grip the outsides of Camden's muscular thighs, while he adjusts himself and then slides his penis into my mouth. Almost immediately I feel another rush of wet heat between my legs. I actually like arrogant Camden King force-feeding his dick into my mouth. *Who knew?* So, surprise surprise, that is yet another one of my rules I'm breaking.

1. No kissing.

2. No fucking the boss.

3. No controlling shit.

4. No fellatio.

Camden begins to gently pump himself in and out of my mouth. Making sure not to move to deeply at first, probably so he doesn't choke me to death. Allowing me to get adjusted to the girth of his cock and the rhythm of his thrusts.

I'm starting to really like this. In fact I want to participate more by at least holding him at the base of his dick or fondling his balls a little, but Camden won't allow it.

"Hands," he reprimands me with a guttural growl

when I try to move them. "Back on my legs. *Yes*, Jade, that feels so fucking good."

It's amazing to me how even with my hands basically tethered to his body, holding onto his thighs, that I still feel totally powerful. That I am completely controlling Camden's pleasure with my mouth and henceforth increasing mine as well.

"Spread your legs."

I hesitate at first. I don't want him to see how wet I am. Even though I am enjoying myself, I still can't get completely out of my head. I never do when I have sex. It's a blessing and a curse.

"Wider," he insists.

I take a hard pull on Camden's dick with my mouth as punishment for reprimanding me, but it has the opposite effect. He loves it. He folds his enormous body completely over on all fours and starts licking and lapping me between my legs while pumping himself harder in and out of my mouth.

We are in a perfect sixty-nine position, and for a split second I'm frightened. Probably because I know that I can't control his thrusts in this position. What if he gets excited? What if he starts ramming himself down my throat and I can't stop him? But as these random concerns for my safety swirl around in my head, I can't deny that with each passing moment I feel good. Better than good. My eyes are practically rolling in the back of my head, as we begin to become lost in each other. A sensual and mutual game of tit for tat.

Every time he flicks my clit with his tongue.

I suck him harder.

Every time I take a stronger pull of his cock.

He takes a powerful one of my clit.

It's almost a battle of wills. Who is going to come first? Who is going to scream for mercy first? He's trying to break me, like I'm some sort of wild stallion, not because I believe that he wants me so badly, but probably because there's never been a woman who's told Camden no in his life.

Maybe I serve as some interesting sort of challenge for him, but he's going to realize quickly that there is no way I am ever going to allow him to break me. I will always be free. I will never surrender and become someone's property, someone's plaything, or someone's ATM machine ever again. But if there was anyone ever able to get me to bend my will, God knows that Camden would be the one.

He lightens up on the suction of my clit. Then he bites it.

Then he kisses gently around my core. Almost reverently.

Then rapidly licks back and forth across my clit with his powerful tongue like a human vibrator.

All while holding my legs spread wide and immobile.

It was all beginning to be too much. I was positive stronger women had fallen for less. My legs were beginning to shake, and I swore I could feel my heart pounding through my chest.

"Come for me, Jade," he demands with urgency.

And I come swift and hard like a wild banshee. Screaming expletives and some other unintelligible words, because it feels just that good. Then he comes inside of my mouth with a hushed curse of his own.

"Fuck."

Hot, salty, lava floods my mouth and drips down my throat, but I swallow every drop and am proud that I do. Now I'm hot and sweaty and still very horny. I want more of Camden. So much more. Like him inside of me all over this hotel room, but I refuse to beg for it. Which is what I'm pretty sure he's looking for me to do. He seems the type to get off on begging.

Camden finally lifts his large body from over me and sits against the headboard of the bed staring at me while stroking my hair. It's an odd gesture, because it seems to be part of the post afterglow that lovers share, not two people just fucking around.

The unforgettable orgasm which has totally rocked my body, has me lying here panting for breath, as if I'm unfit and don't run a couple of miles everyday. It must have been the erotic mixture of exertion, adrenaline and bliss making me unusually winded. I can honestly say that no man has ever made me come that hard. I'm already bemoaning the fact that this one-night stand is going to be difficult to put behind me.

"I want to fuck you, Jade, but I'm not going to have my dick inside of you on a Saturday and another man's in there on a Monday."

When he put it that way, he made me sound like a whore, and maybe I was a little, but I liked it that way. Dictating whom I had sex with. Calling the shots about where. Always in charge of the when. Not feeling stifled by relationship restrictions or expectations. And never being disappointed by disappointing men. Yeah, if I had to choose between being a whore and being a pushover then I pick whore all day.

"I'm not sure what you're trying to say."

"It's not a difficult concept. If I'm fucking you,

then you're only fucking me."

"Well you're not fucking only me, you're fucking me *tonight*, there's a difference."

He glares at me with icy eyes.

"What are you doing in Baltimore, Jade?"

"Why do you keep asking me that? What do you think I'm doing here?"

"I don't fucking know!" he roars. "That's why I'm asking."

"Huh, you seem upset. I guess all of your little computer programs could track me here, but couldn't tell you *why* I was here. Is that the problem?"

He rubs his face harshly with the palm of his hand in frustration.

"Run the Jacuzzi water again."

"Why?"

"You're going to need it," he says with a maniacal hunger in his eyes I've never seen before.

"I thought you needed assurances that I wouldn't be fucking anyone tomorrow, or the next day, or the next—"

He quiets me with his mouth again.

This time with much more urgency.

And I welcome it.

The warmth of his tongue caressing mine.

A girl could get used to it even though she shouldn't.

"I've decided that I don't want you to make me any empty promises or pledges right now."

He pulls back from the kiss to look directly at me when he speaks.

"Because after tonight you won't want anyone inside of you but me. That I can *assure* you."

Want to find out what happens next?
TAP TO DOWNLOAD THE BOOK INSTANTLY

MY VIP LIST (Get the nitty gritty)
I have a VIP Reader mailing list. I only send free books, new release, sales or special giveaway information to this group. No spam. You can join here: http://LisaLangBlakeney.com/VIP

MY PRIVATE FAN GROUP (Casual fun)
Join my private Fan Group on Facebook also known as my "Romance Ninja Warriors" where I share all things new going on, celebrate birthdays, post teasers, yummy pics, giveaways and just chit chat. http://LisaLangBlakeney.com/community

THE ARC TEAM (Book Reviewers)

If you are interested in joining my beta reader team then please join here: https://geni.us/N8jAU

Bronx - Bronx & Karma

The King Brothers Series
Dive into this series of interconnected standalones
featuring 3 alpha hot brothers and the women they
lay claim to without apology.
Claimed - Camden & Jade
Indebted - Cutter & Sloan
Broken - Stone & Tiny
Promised - All King Brothers
King Brothers Box Set

The Nighthawk Series
Sexy & sweet sports romances set in the professional
world of football. All standalones.
Saint - Saint & Sabrina
Wolf - Cooper & Ursula
Diesel - Mason & Olivia
Jett - Jett & Adrienne
Rush - Rush & Mia

Lisa Lang Blakeney is a USA Today Bestselling author of contemporary romance sold in more than 28 countries. Worried that her fellow PTO moms might disapprove, she wrote and published her steamy debut novel Masterson under a different title and pen name in August of 2015.

Thanks to strong reader support of her alpha male character, Roman Masterson, she was encouraged to continue with the series and published the entire Masterson Trilogy the following year. She hasn't looked back since and continues to write novels featuring strong alpha men and the smart women they seek to claim.

A romance junkie for sure, you can find Lisa watching a romantic comedy, reading a romance novel, or writing one of her own most days of the week. If she's not doing that, she's outside in the garden tending to her roses.

Lisa is the wife of one alpha (whom she met in college), mother to four girls, and two labradoodles. Get news on releases, sales and giveaways when you become one of Lisa's VIP readers at : http:// LisaLangBlakeney.com/VIP

facebook.com/authorlisalangblakeney

twitter.com/LisaLangWrites

instagram.com/LisaLangBlakeney

amazon.com/author/lisalangblakeney

bookbub.com/authors/lisa-lang-blakeney

goodreads.com/Lisa_Lang_Blakeney

pinterest.com/lisalangwrites

tiktok.com/@lisalangblakeney

patreon.com/lisalangblakeney